# PANAMA

*by*
*Gail B. Stewart*

## CRESTWOOD HOUSE
New York

Collier Macmillan Canada
Toronto

..l Macmillan International Publishing Group
New York  Oxford  Singapore  Sydney

**Library of Congress Cataloging-in-Publication Data**
Stewart, Gail, 1949-
  Panama/ by Gail B. Stewart. — 1st ed.
    p.  cm. — (Places in the news)
  Includes index.
  Summary: Examines historical and recent events that have kept Panama in the news.
  ISBN 0-89686-536-3
  1. Panama—History—Juvenile literature. 2. Panama Canal (Panama)—History—Juvenile literature.
3. Panama—Relations—United States—Juvenile literature. 4. United States—Relations—Panama—Juvenile
literature. [1. Panama—Relations—United States. 2. United States—Relations—Panama. 3. Panama—History.]
I. Title. II. Series: Stewart, Gail, 1949-  Places in the news.
F1566.S86   1990
972.87—dc20                                                          90-36249
                                                                         CIP
                                                                          AC

**Photo Credits**
Cover: Magnum Photos, Inc.: Susan Meiselas
AP—Wide World Photos: 4, 7, 20, 23, 26, 29, 32, 36, 43
Culver Pictures, Inc.: 13
Magnum Photos, Inc.: (Susan Meiselas) 16
Journalism Services: (Scott Defries) 39

Macmillan Publishing Company          Collier Macmillan Canada, Inc.
866 Third Avenue                      1200 Eglinton Avenue East
New York, NY  10022                   Suite 200
                                      Don Mills, Ontario M3C 3N1

CRESTWOOD HOUSE

Produced by Flying Fish Studio Incorporated

Printed in the United States of America

First Edition

10 9 8 7 6 5 4 3 2 1

# CONTENTS

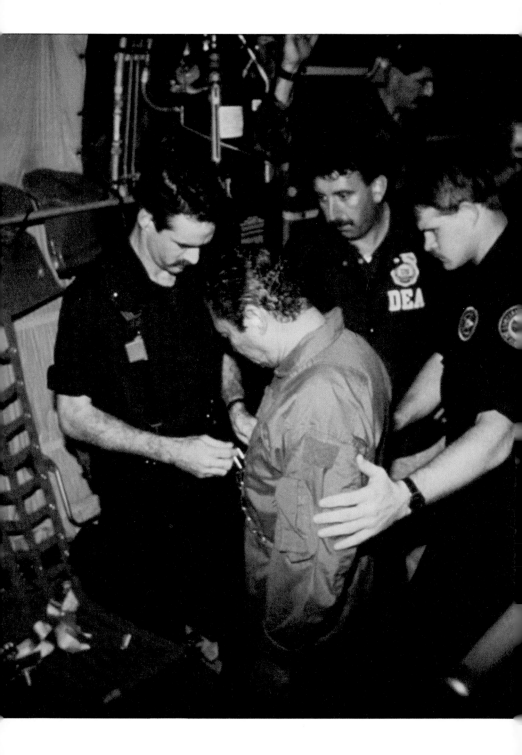

# PANAMA
# IN THE NEWS

On January 10, 1990, newspaper headlines all over the world carried the news: Panama's leader, Manuel Antonio Noriega, had been arrested by the United States government.

It is very unusual for the leader of a country to be arrested by another country. The United States had been watching Noriega for a long time. According to U.S. officials, his crimes were severe.

Two years earlier, U.S. drug enforcement agents say, they learned that Noriega was involved in the smuggling of cocaine and marijuana. Drug smugglers frequently use small planes to fly drugs from Colombia, where the drugs are grown and processed. No small plane can carry enough fuel to fly nonstop to the United States, so Panama was a useful midway point. Noriega is said to have accepted millions of dollars in bribes from Colombian drug lords to protect these shipments of drugs.

Noriega has been accused of assisting drug traffickers in other ways, as well. He is said to have supplied chemicals to the secret laboratories that turn coca leaves into cocaine. He has been accused of helping drug traffickers deposit their profits into legitimate bank accounts that cannot be traced by law enforcement officials. Called laundering, this process is important to drug traffickers, for it hides the huge sums of money they earn illegally.

*In January 1990, Panama's General Manuel Noriega was arrested by the U.S. government on drug trafficking charges.*

Drug trafficking is not the only wrongdoing of which Panama's leader has been accused. He ignored the results of an election in 1989 that would have stripped him of power. Instead of accepting the decision of the voters, Noriega sent his soldiers to attack the winning candidate.

The list of Noriega's crimes—affecting Panama, the United States, and other nations—was a long one. One American spokesperson said that Noriega posed "a grave threat to the United States and other countries."

President George Bush gave the order to invade Panama on December 20, and the troops surrounded Noriega's headquarters. However, Noriega managed to evade them, and on Christmas Eve he took refuge in the Vatican embassy.

Throughout history, churches have been considered havens for anyone, criminal or not. Churches have declared themselves outside the jurisdiction, or power, of police and other law enforcement people. For this reason, Noriega was safe while he remained in the embassy.

Although the U.S. soldiers outside the embassy could do nothing to capture Noriega, they applied some pressure. Day and night, they yelled at Noriega's window. They set up loudspeakers and blared rock music at the embassy 24 hours a day. The songs—such as "No Place to Hide" and "You're No Good"—were carefully chosen, too.

Crowds of Panamanians gathered outside the embassy, as well. They chanted anti-Noriega slogans and held up signs criticizing the leader.

Finally Noriega could hold out no longer. Church officials had talked to him, explaining that it would be more honorable for him

*United States soldiers wait outside the Vatican embassy, where Noriega sought refuge after the U.S. invasion in December 1989. Church officials eventually convinced Noriega to surrender.*

to face up to the charges against him. U.S. officials promised he would not face the death penalty for drug charges.

# *Prisoner*

When he finally walked out of the embassy, Noriega was very quiet. This was quite a change from the talkative, aggressive way he usually acted in public. U.S. soldiers clicked handcuffs around his wrists. He was ordered to remove his four-star-general's uniform. In its place, he was given a drab air force flight suit to wear.

U.S. officials read Noriega his rights in Spanish. He boarded the bulky C-130 cargo plane that took him to Miami, Florida. When he arrived at the prison in Miami, he was treated the same as other prisoners. Even though he had been the leader of Panama, he got no special treatment. Noriega has argued strongly against this. He claims he should be considered a prisoner of war. But so far, Noriega is just prisoner number 41586.

Panama has stayed in the news even after Noriega's surrender. The nation is going through difficult times. Panamanians are now trying to get used to a new government. Their new president, Guillermo Endara, is supported (some say even appointed) by the United States. But he still must prove to his people that he is more than just "Noriega's replacement."

Although some people applauded the United States decision to invade Panama, many others criticized it. They have questioned whether the United States has the right to invade a nation with which it is not at war. They also wonder if it is illegal to imprison the leader of another country—especially if he did not commit any crimes in the United States.

President Bush, however, has reminded critics that there are many Americans living in Panama. These Americans had to be protected, said President Bush, especially since Noriega had made threats against them. That was one of the reasons for the U.S. invasion.

Panama is important to the United States and has been since the beginning of the 20th century. It is the location of the most important waterway connecting the Atlantic Ocean with the Pacific Ocean—the Panama Canal. Because of the canal, Panama and the United States are bound very closely. The relationship between the two countries has its roots in the Panama Canal.

# *FROM THE BEGINNING*

The area now known as Panama is important because of its location. Geographers are people who study the physical features of the earth. They call Panama an isthmus. That means it is a narrow strip of land connecting two large masses of land. In the case of Panama, the two large masses are North America and South America.

9

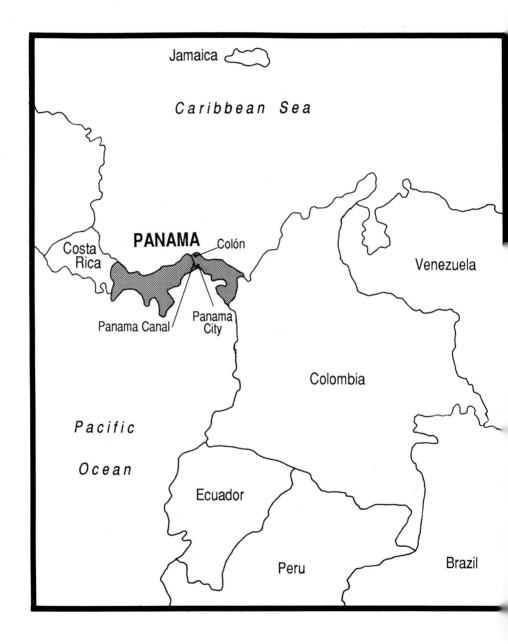

Jamaica

*Caribbean Sea*

Costa
Rica

**PANAMA**　Colón

Panama Canal　Panama
City

Venezuela

Colombia

*Pacific*

*Ocean*

Ecuador

Peru

Brazil

At the beginning of this century, the United States built a canal through that strip of land for its own use. The canal was built so American ships could go between the Atlantic and Pacific oceans faster than ever. For that reason, the United States has been in charge of its operation. However, the United States was not the first country to use Panama for its own gain.

# Searching for Gold

Spanish explorers came to the isthmus in the early 16th century. The Spanish were interested in two things: gold and new territory to claim for Spain. They encountered tribes of natives who lived by hunting in the jungles and fishing off the coasts.

The Spanish established a home base at an Indian fishing village. They named the place "Panama." The word means "plenty of fish."

The settlers eventually did discover gold, but not in Panama. Beginning in the 1500s, and continuing until the late 1700s, they found vast treasures of gold and other valuables. Most of it came from Peru, to the south. The Spanish took these treasures from the great civilization of the Incas. Although they outnumbered the Spaniards, the Incas were conquered fairly easily. The Spaniards had advanced weapons and methods of warfare. After conquering the Incas, the Spaniards claimed their gold, silver, and emeralds.

The Spaniards could not load the treasure into their ships in Peru, for that country bordered the Pacific Ocean. The Pacific lay on the opposite shore and was the route to China and the East. To get back to Spain, a ship had to sail on the Atlantic.

The solution for the Spaniards was to move their treasure up through Colombia into Panama. Ships laden with treasure could easily sail from Panama back to Spain. For two centuries, the Spaniards used this route. After a while, they even built a road between Panama and Peru. It was quite narrow—only seven feet wide. They called it The Royal Road.

# Independence from Spain

Panama and its neighbor to the south, Colombia, were colonies of Spain. The Spanish did not rule the territories wisely, however. They did not allow the colonists to make any of their own decisions. Spain also put many restrictions on the kind of trade the colonies could do.

Colombia fought off Spanish control first, in 1819. Panama got its independence from Spain two years later. At the same time, Panama decided to become part of the larger country of Colombia. For 82 years, it stayed that way. Panama did not become independent from Colombia until 1903, with the help of the United States.

# Valuable Once More

In 1849 Panama became as important to Americans as it had been to the Spanish in the 16th century. Gold again played a big part—but not the gold of the Incas. This time it was the discovery of gold in California!

*With their suits of armor and strong swords, the early Spanish explorers easily conquered native Panamanian tribes.*

13

Thousands of people in America were eager to journey to California to find their fortunes. Most were from the East Coast of the United States. There were three ways these forty-niners, as the miners came to be called, could travel from the East Coast to California.

The first was to join a wagon train heading west. That was a frightening and dangerous way to travel. The territory was unfamiliar and inhabited by hostile Native Americans and wild animals. Stories abounded of people who never survived this overland trip.

The second way was just as dangerous. It was a sea voyage that began at an eastern port such as New York and continued all the way around South America to San Francisco. Any sea voyage of that length was risky, but this trip was especially so. There were treacherous currents off Cape Horn, the southern tip of South America, where the Atlantic meets the Pacific. The seas were rough, and dangerous storms made navigation tricky. Many ships were lost in heavy fog and crashed on the rocks of the cape.

The third choice forty-niners had in getting to California was a combination of ocean and land travel. They could get on a ship in New York and sail to Panama and then make their way across Panama, probably on the old Royal Road. When they had crossed to the Pacific side of Panama, they could get on another ship and sail up to California!

The trip was long and difficult, but to many hopeful miners, it was worth it. More and more forty-niners each year decided to go by way of Panama.

# A Moneymaking Railroad

Although the route across Panama was becoming a popular shortcut, there were still a great many dangers along the way. Travelers found it difficult to hack their way through the hilly jungles of Panama—even using The Royal Road. The weather was steamy and hot, and mud and rain made the journey very unpleasant. There were poisonous insects and swarms of mosquitoes. Worst of all, the mosquitoes carried diseases such as malaria and yellow fever, which killed many travelers.

Even with these dangers, however, travelers continued to use the Panama shortcut. That's when some Americans had the idea of building a railroad across the isthmus. It would help travelers cross the jungles of Panama more safely and help the railroad builders get rich.

The railroad took five years to build. Even though Americans had the idea, they did not build it themselves. They used cheap labor—Chinese immigrants, Native Americans, and the descendants of African slaves, all of whom did not have enough power to demand fair wages.

More than six thousand men died—mostly from malaria and yellow fever—building the railroad. In fact, malaria killed workers in a number of ways. Some died from the disease itself. Others became depressed (one of the aftereffects of malaria) and killed themselves.

At this high human cost, the railroad was completed in 1855. The line linked Colón on the Atlantic side and Panama City on the Pacific side. The trip was about 47 miles and took a little over four

hours. It was expensive, too—25 gold dollars for a one-way ticket.

Those Americans who invested in the Panama railroad made a great deal of money. The project was costly—the final total was $8 million. However, in the first six years of operation, the railroad took in $7 million in profits!

Panama prospered during the time of the railroad. However, in 1869 a railroad was built in the United States connecting East and West. No longer was it necessary to take two sea trips as well as the overland one. The building of the transcontinental railroad seemed to mark the end of Panama's new prosperity.

# Can It Be Done?

There was no longer a need for Panama's railroad. However, there was interest in digging a canal through the isthmus. A waterway joining the Atlantic and the Pacific had always been the dream of sailors. In fact, the explorer Alexander von Humboldt had drawn up plans for a waterway back in 1811. He had decided Panama would be the most logical place, since the isthmus was so narrow. However, at the time, the technology to complete a canal did not exist.

By the late 1800s, however, people had gained the technical knowledge. The United States Navy was excited about the idea. Valuable time could be saved with a canal, especially during war. And merchants who depended on trade ships longed for a shortcut, too. With a canal through Central America, it would take far less time for goods to travel from one market to another.

*The Panama Canal connects the Atlantic and Pacific oceans.*
*It plays a vital role in U.S. defense and trade.*

It was a Frenchman, however, who finally began the project. He was Ferdinand Marie de Lesseps. Lesseps recently had made a name for himself by digging a canal in Egypt, called the Suez Canal. A French-owned company asked for permission to dig through Panama. It asked Colombia, since Panama was still part of that country. Colombia agreed to sell the land, and the French began digging in 1882.

# No Use

The world watched the progress of the Panama Canal with interest. Lesseps and his assistants planned most of the project carefully and carried out some of it efficiently. However, they encountered even more problems than the builders of the railroad had.

Epidemics of tropical diseases hit the workers. Historians tell us that for every 100 men who worked on the canal, 20 died. When Lesseps finally quit seven years later, 16,000 men had died. Besides the high death toll, other problems caused the project to fail. Dishonest politicians who backed Lesseps stole a lot of money from the canal company. And the French engineers lacked the proper tools to complete such a huge digging job. By 1889 only 10 percent of the canal had been dug, but it was simply no use to continue.

# The Nicaragua Canal?

Even though the French had failed, many people in the United States refused to give up the idea. A canal was a good idea, many thought, but perhaps Panama was the wrong place to build it.

Some—including many in Congress—thought Nicaragua would make a better spot. After all, they argued, Nicaragua was closer to the United States. It would be easier to maintain control over the canal. The climate, too, was better in Nicaragua. It was not as sticky and hot as in Panama. The government of Nicaragua also seemed more stable. It was very risky to do business with an unstable area like Panama, which was on the brink of revolution with Colombia.

As it turned out, of course, Nicaragua wasn't chosen. One of the main reasons was that it had nine active volcanoes. That seemed even more of a risk than all of Panama's shortcomings put together!

# THE UNITED STATES BUILDS A CANAL

Today distrust and anger sour the relations between many Central American nations and the United States—an unfortunate state of affairs for such close neighbors. Many of these hard feelings, experts on Central America say, began with the Panama Canal.

# Independence for Panama

The beginning of the 20th century held great promise for the United States. New inventions such as the automobile and the telephone were making life more exciting. The nation was expanding, too. Hawaii had recently been added, or annexed. The country had just won the Spanish-American War. New territories such as Guam, Puerto Rico, and the Philippines were under U.S. control.

It was called the Age of Optimism. People were sure the future would be as great as the present. The president was an aggressive, outgoing man named Teddy Roosevelt. He was eager to keep America on the move. The existence of a canal would be another step forward.

Before building a canal, the United States had to get permission from Colombia. But Colombia did not want to give the United States rights to such a project. Colombian officials realized what a large money-maker a canal could be. They had no reason to turn such a prime piece of land over to the United States.

President Roosevelt was furious. He urged Colombian leaders to reconsider, but they would not. He wrote a letter to his secretary of state, calling the officials of Colombia "a bunch of jackrabbits." The only hope for the canal project, he insisted, would be for Panama to get its independence. The people of Panama were enthusiastic and would surely approve the canal.

On November 3, 1903, Roosevelt got his wish. The people of Panama revolted against Colombia. The United States not only lent moral support; it assisted in the rebellion.

*President Theodore Roosevelt helped Panama gain independence from Colombia. In exchange, Panama signed a treaty allowing the United States to build and control the canal.*  21

Colombia refused to accept Panama's declaration of independence. Colombian officials sent troops to Panama to put down
the rebellion. The United States, however, had sent marines to
Panama to keep Colombia from doing just that!

Colombian soldiers had to travel from Colón to Panama City,
the center of the revolution. But U.S. officials would not let them
use the Panama railroad. Only Colombia's generals and admirals
were allowed on the train. No troops were permitted to get to the
rebels in Panama City. When the train pulled in to Panama City,
large crowds cheered and bands played. The generals and admirals were seized and put into jail.

The United States helped Panama in another way, as well. In
a silent "show of strength," President Roosevelt ordered a large
gunboat to sail into Panama's harbor. The USS *Nashville* did not
fire a shot, but the Colombians got the message. They knew that
Panama had American support. The Colombians did not have a
chance against such a powerful nation.

# *"Gunboat Diplomacy"*

The United States was not respected for its actions in Panama.
Instead, many nations throughout the world criticized what it had
done.

Colombians were angriest of all. What right had the United
States to interfere in their country? they asked. The United States

*In 1903 the United States showed its support for Panama's independence from Colombia by sending the USS* Nashville *(shown here being launched) into Panama's harbor.*

had signed a treaty with Colombia in 1846. The treaty stated that the United States would protect Colombia's claim to Panama. In exchange, U.S. citizens and soldiers would be allowed to cross the isthmus freely. But now that treaty had been violated. The United States had meddled in an uprising in another country. That was neither fair nor right, Colombia argued, and many other countries of the world agreed.

The nations of Central America let their feelings be known. Historians say that there was a sense of outrage about the way the United States had conducted itself. Critics used the term "gunboat diplomacy" to describe America's actions. It refers to the way the United States intimidated other countries to get its own way.

# One-Sided Agreement

President Roosevelt and other U.S. officials moved quickly once Panama became independent. They signed a treaty on November 18, 1903, with a representative from Panama.

The treaty was extremely one-sided in favor of the United States. Even Roosevelt's supporters were surprised at how much Panama gave up in the agreement.

The treaty called for the United States to pay Panama $10 million. Beginning in 1913, the United States would pay an annual fee of $250,000 to Panama for the use of the canal. This must have sounded like a lot of money to the new leaders of Panama. After all, theirs was a brand-new government, with absolutely no money. But the United States was the big winner in the deal.

According to the treaty, the United States would pay for the canal. It would have control over the canal and of the land five miles on either side of the canal. This area would be called the Canal Zone. It would not be considered part of Panama any longer. It would be totally controlled by the United States. The phrase "in perpetuity" was used to describe how long the agreement would last. "In perpetuity" means forever.

# Getting the Job Done

The United States soon began digging the canal. The story of the building of the canal is a remarkable one. It was one of the most difficult projects ever undertaken. Many people endured the worst conditions imaginable while digging the canal. Thousands lost their lives.

In the end, though, the project succeeded because of great engineers such as David Gaillard. They figured out how to cut huge excavations through mountains—an almost impossible task. Yet it was not only the engineers who made the project a success.

Historians agree that without the medical genius of Dr. William Gorgas, the United States would have had to abandon the project, just as the French had. Gorgas discovered that the deadly diseases killing workers were caused by mosquitoes. The insects carried germs and infected anyone they stung. And in the hot,

The building of the canal took ten years and cost over $380 million. It took the lives of thousands of workers, who died from malaria and other tropical diseases.

humid climate of Panama, mosquitoes were everywhere! Once this was understood, workers were able to take steps to prevent the insects from hatching.

It took ten years to dig the canal. The first ship passed through the canal on August 15, 1914. It cost the United States more than $380 million to complete the canal. However, in terms of the respect and trust the United States lost from its neighbors, the cost was much higher.

# TROUBLE IN PANAMA

Some Panamanians were angry about the canal from the beginning. As the years went by, more and more people voiced their dissatisfaction. They thought the United States controlled far too much and that Panama had been paid far too little.

## Flags Above the Canal Zone

Discontent grew especially intense in the 1950s, when people in Panama protested against the United States. The demonstrators objected to the idea of the Canal Zone. Why should the United States completely control an area that is really part of Panama? they asked.

The United States was aware of the unrest. To smooth over the hostility, the United States offered to pay more money to Panama. The United States raised the yearly payment from $250,000 to $1.9 million. After all, the United States was collecting millions of dollars in tolls every year from ships using the canal.

The money issue was only one of the reasons the Panamanians were angry. In 1958 and again in 1962, questions were raised about the flags in the Canal Zone. Many in Panama thought it was wrong for the U.S. flag to wave alone over the zone, as if Panama did not exist. Demonstrations against the United States grew violent.

In 1964 a riot erupted in Panama. American students tried to fly the American flag above their school. Fighting broke out, and troops were called in. By the time the rioting was over, twenty-one Panamanians and four U.S. soldiers were dead.

Panama's president, Roberto Chiari, was furious. He made a speech in which he called the United States "barbaric." He also declared that from that moment, Panama would break off all relations with the United States. The two nations would have nothing more to do with each other.

# A New Agreement

When the United Nations saw the hostility between the United States and Panama, it urged the two countries to try to get along. The United Nations is an organization that is committed to world peace. United Nations officials from around the world told Panama to keep the lines of communication open.

In 1977 U.S. President Jimmy Carter met with Panamanian President Omar Torrijos. They signed a new agreement giving Panama full control of the canal.

The two nations agreed to try. However, they were not able to come to terms until 1977. In a historic meeting, U.S. President Jimmy Carter and Panama's President Omar Torrijos signed two new agreements. Their 1977 treaties have replaced the original one signed in 1903.

One new treaty abolishes the Canal Zone. There is no "country within a country" controlled by the United States. The canal is now simply part of the nation of Panama. This treaty also gives Panama ownership of the canal. The ownership will come gradually. By the year 2000, the nation of Panama will have complete responsibility for the canal.

The other treaty gives the United States the right to defend the canal's neutrality. This means the United States could send armed forces to the area if it thought that the canal was threatened by a foreign power.

Currently the canal employs 3,500 American workers and more than 10,000 Panamanians. The head of the canal has always been an American. The second-in-command, called the deputy, has been a Panamanian. On January 1, 1990, a step toward Panamanian control was made. The head of the canal and the deputy changed places. From now on, the top official will always be a Panamanian.

# America's Concern

Many Americans agreed with the treaty. They believed that the United States was doing the right thing in giving the canal back to Panama. However, there were some who felt that it was too risky. And today there are people who still feel that way.

These critics do not find fault with the idea of giving the canal to Panama. They are concerned that the canal be managed correctly. Their worry is whether Panama will have a government strong and stable enough to protect the canal.

If Panama became a communist country, or was run by people hostile to the United States, what then? Critics fear the hard work and money spent building and maintaining the canal would go to waste. Ships from the United States use the canal all the time. Some of the ships carry millions of tons of American goods overseas. Some are navy ships, protecting the waters around North America.

If Panama stopped being friendly with the United States, its leaders might forbid American ships to use the canal. Merchants would suffer, as well as American defense.

# The Panamanian Government

In 1977 Panama seemed to have a fairly stable government. However, recent events in Panama have made top U.S. officials nervous.

Panama has a democratic form of government, as does the United States. According to Panama's constitution, the head of the government is the president. The people in Panama elect the president and vice president.

However, the government works differently in real life. The

*Like other Panamanian dictators before him, Manuel Noriega rose to power by gaining control of Panama's National Guard.*

real power behind Panama's government is the National Guard. The National Guard is made up of soldiers whose job is to keep peace.

The head of the National Guard is always a general. It is that general who holds all the real power in Panama. If that general does not approve of a president—even though that president has been elected by the people—the president will not remain in office long. The general of the National Guard can use whatever means he has to urge the president to resign.

Therefore, the security of Panama—and the canal—rests with the general of the National Guard. If he is honest and responsible, the critics of the 1977 treaty have nothing to worry about. However, that has not been the case.

# *Manuel Antonio Noriega*

In 1983 General Manuel Antonio Noriega became the head of the National Guard in Panama. Until his arrest by U.S. officials in January 1990, Noriega was the most powerful man in Panama.

During his years in power, Noriega did things that troubled many U.S. government leaders. He seemed to be neither honest nor responsible. U.S. officials were concerned about the future of the canal. For that reason, they watched Noriega's activities carefully.

Many Americans got their first look at Noriega in May 1989. Panama was in the headlines quite a bit at that time. An important government election was being held, and Noriega was involved.

# *Challenging Noriega's Power*

Noriega was not actually running for office. In 1989 he was in full control of Panama. He had so much power, in fact, that he was a dictator. That means that he was the only real authority in the nation. Everyone had to obey his wishes.

But 1989 was the scheduled year for presidential elections. Even though the president would not have much real power, the elections had to be held.

Some people in Panama wanted to end Noriega's power. Their leader was Guillermo Endara. Endara and his supporters hoped that they could challenge Noriega's authority. To do that, they would have to beat the candidate Noriega had chosen to run.

Officials from other nations went to Panama to observe the elections. This happens sometimes when there might be some cheating. A panel of impartial observers helps count votes. That way, the results of the election can be trusted.

Noriega felt very confident that his candidate would win and that he would still be dictator. He was so sure, in fact, that he agreed to let a panel of observers come to Panama.

# *A Bloody Election*

Two former U.S. presidents were part of this panel—Jimmy Carter and Gerald Ford—along with government representatives from other democratic nations.

As the results of the voting began coming in, Noriega was

alarmed. He had been far off in his predictions. Instead of being ahead of Endara, his candidate was losing by a 3-to-1 margin.

Noriega hurriedly gave members of the National Guard special voting cards. These cards allowed them to vote in any district, as often as they wanted. However, Noriega thought even more drastic measures had to be taken.

He ordered members of the National Guard to seize voting tally sheets. They delivered phony tally sheets to the central election headquarters—sheets that showed Noriega's side to be winning. National Guard troops used force on election workers, too. They used guns and clubs to beat up anyone who objected to their methods.

People around the world watched the news on television in disbelief. They saw squads of Noriega's men moving through crowds, beating people with tire irons and knives. These squads, easily spotted in their bright red-and-blue T-shirts, attacked people for voting against Noriega.

Endara and his running mates were also beaten up. As the candidates waved to supporters from the back of a pickup truck, Noriega's men dragged them out. The candidates were struck with fists, knives, guns, and clubs. Endara, his shirt torn and bloody, was rushed to a hospital. He had a deep cut in his scalp.

The panel members were outraged. One official from Australia called the election "a complete fraud." Former President Carter urged people around the world to condemn Noriega and his vicious followers.

The Panamanian government declared that the election was "null and void." It accused the foreign officials of tampering with Panama's government. Power, at least for the time being, stayed with Noriega alone.

*Noriega remained in power by controlling all of the elections in Panama. He used threats and violence to make people afraid to vote against his candidates.*

# THE FALL OF NORIEGA

By not allowing fair elections in Panama, Noriega was breaking the laws of his country. However, the May election in Panama was just one of the incidents that alarmed U.S. officials.

Intelligence agencies in the United States had been watching Noriega for many years. They say they had evidence of his drug trafficking as well as other serious crimes. Yet, because he was dictator, he could not be arrested or put in jail. He controlled the police as well as the military.

## What to Do about Noriega

It was difficult for President Bush to solve the problem of Noriega. On the one hand, General Noriega was responsible for millions of dollars' worth of drugs entering the United States. And he was not allowing his government to operate in a fair, democratic way.

On the other hand, how could the United States get involved? Panama is not part of the United States. It is a foreign nation. How could the United States go into another nation and arrest its leader? The outrage Central America felt in 1903 when the United States helped Panama against Colombia would rise to the surface again.

Invading Panama did not seem like a good option. U.S.

officials knew that such a move would break international law and order. Other nations would condemn the United States.

One way a nation can punish another is by using economic sanctions. When a nation imposes economic sanctions on another, it refuses to trade or do business with that nation. All economic ties are cut. The goal of economic sanctions is to make the nation suffer. Less money and fewer products go to that nation, so its economy suffers. The people then put pressure on their government to change.

However, sanctions did not work in Panama. The United States cut off aid, and the Panamanian economy declined. Once the most active trading nation in Latin America, Panama did suffer. Unemployment levels rose: About one in five Panamanians was out of work. However, Noriega himself was not affected. He continued to make a great deal of money from drug trafficking. In fact, estimates of Noriega's wealth are in the hundreds of millions.

# Invading Panama

In the months after the May election, Noriega's military forces became more hostile. Americans living and working in Panama were threatened and, in some cases, beaten. Noriega himself said that "a state of war exists between Panama and the United States."

On December 16, a U.S. Marine lieutenant was killed by Panamanians. The United States called the incident "an unprovoked attack."

*U.S. troops under fire during the invasion of Panama in December 1989*

Citing these reasons, as well as Noriega's drug trafficking, President Bush gave the go-ahead for an invasion. On December 20, U.S. troops invaded Panama City. They surrounded Noriega's headquarters. The general, however, escaped, and did not surrender to American forces until January 10, 1990.

# Some Disturbing Questions

The U.S. invasion of Panama and the arrest of Noriega have raised some difficult questions. Many people around the world, as well as in the United States, wonder whether the invasion was just.

Some officials in Central America were very angry. "It's a very tricky situation," one diplomat from Ecuador said. "No one liked Noriega—you would have a hard time finding any nation who would stand by him. On the other hand, while everyone is glad he's gone, we just wonder: Who gives the United States the right?"

Many people in America feel the same way. They feel that there is a double standard at work. As one political expert remarked, "The United States has, through history, given itself the right to interfere in Central America. We as a nation can set up their governments. We can direct their economies. We can even move in with our army when their leaders break the law. But can you imagine what we would say if Panama sent in troops to Washington if our president were committing crimes?"

There are many, too, who defend the president's decision. They believe that, because American lives were in danger, the United States had every right to protect them.

# Whose Side Was He On?

As more information about Noriega comes to light, people see that the issue is more complicated than it first appeared. In late January 1990, the U.S. government admitted a startling fact. For years, General Noriega had worked for U.S. intelligence agencies when George Bush was their director. In other words, the U.S. government did not always treat him as a villain. Instead, it supported him for a long time.

In fact, Noriega was paid a salary of $110,000 per year. He was paid to supply information. Some of the information was about secret agents. Some information had to do with the activities of other nations. Noriega had information about Nicaragua, Colombia, and Communist activity in Central America. And at the same time that he was handing information to the United States, he was doing the same for other nations! Cuba, Nicaragua, and El Salvador were just some of the countries that received secrets from Noriega.

Four U.S. presidents, over a period of 20 years, knew about Noriega's crimes. Nixon, Ford, Carter, and Reagan all knew of his drug dealing and other illegal activities. Yet, it seems, they chose not to act. "At the time, it seemed that Noriega's intelligence was even better than ours," admitted one U.S. intelligence agent. "It was a matter of priorities. We needed his information, and we were willing to overlook an awful lot to get it. It may be coming back to haunt us now."

# *What Lies Ahead?*

After Noriega was taken into custody, a new president of Panama was sworn in. He is Guillermo Endara, the man who ran against Noriega's candidate in the bloody May election.

Although the United States supports him, others are not so sure he should be in office. He was sworn in at a U.S. military base as the invasion was going on, without the approval of Panama's people. Many Panamanians say they are not as supportive of him as they were in May 1989. One banker in Panama remarked that Endara has a MADE IN U.S.A. label on him.

The label is not a very positive thing, at least in Central America. The invasion may have accomplished its goal of getting rid of Noriega. Most Panamanians are glad he is gone. However, the invasion was very destructive. Lives were lost. Thousands of people in Panama City are homeless because their houses were bombed or burned in the fighting.

As time goes by, we will be hearing about them and their former leader. The general is due to stand trial on drug charges in the United States. We will see how Panama rebuilds itself from the destruction caused by Noriega as well as by the United States.

*After the invasion, Guillermo Endara was sworn in as the new president of Panama. He will have to work very hard to repair the damage done by Noriega and his supporters.*

In addition, some interesting questions will need answers. Will the United States continue to influence the affairs of Central American nations? Will the investment of the Panama Canal be safe with Panama's new leaders? And how will these events affect America's relationships with other nations?

# FACTS ABOUT PANAMA

Capital: Panama City

Population: 2.3 million (1989 estimate)

Form of government: Republic, with popular vote

Official languages: Spanish and English

Chief products:
  Agriculture: bananas, rice, coffee, sugarcane, shrimp
  Manufacturing: food processing, beverages, petroleum
    products

# *Glossary*

**annexed** *Added.*

**bribes** *Money or favors given to people to influence their judgment or conduct.*

**dictator** *A ruler with total control of a country.*

**double standard** *A set of principles applying differently to one group than to another.*

**drug traffickers** *Those who transport illegal drugs from one place to another.*

**economic sanctions** *A means of punishing a country by stopping trade and other relations with it.*

**forty-niners** *Those who rushed to California beginning in 1849 to search for gold.*

**geographer** *One who studies the physical features of land.*

**gunboat diplomacy** *The use or threat of military force to gain one's way.*

**isthmus** *A thin strip of land connecting two larger masses of land.*

**jurisdiction** *The limits or territory within which authority may be exercised.*

**laundering** *Hiding sums of money by putting illegal profits into legitimate bank accounts.*

**transcontinental** *Crossing a continent.*

# Index